Daddy's
Hugs and Snuggles

by
Linda Ashman

illustrated by
Jane Massey

cartwheel books™
an imprint of
■SCHOLASTIC

Daddy wakes before I rise.
Drinks his coffee.
Rubs his eyes.

Sees me standing on the stair.
Picks me up.
Smooths my hair.

He makes my breakfast.
Takes a seat.
Reads the news while I eat.

Lifts me up on his knee.
Shows the funny parts to me.

Daddy runs at my side.
Keeps me steady as I ride.

Holds me firm on bumpy ground.
Helps me up when I fall down.

Daddy digs. Daddy weeds.
Hands me tools and pumpkin seeds.

Side by side, we plant the rows.
Soak them gently with the hose.

Daddy listens when I talk.
Lets me linger on a walk.

Lifts me high so I can see.
Makes me laugh.
Laughs with me.

Daddy measures, chops, and rolls.
Lets me pour and stir the bowls.

Fills my plate,
And my cup.
Then we sit and eat it up.

Daddy kneels at the tub.

Sails my boat.

Sinks my sub.

Helps me wash.

Gets me dressed.

Says, "Okay, it's time to rest."

Daddy reads strong and clear.

Asks me questions.

Holds me near.

Gives me kisses.

Tucks me in.

Pulls the blanket to my chin.

Daddy sits
Beside my bed.
Rests his hand upon my head.

Hums a tune, slow and deep,
Till I'm drifting off to sleep.

Just before he turns to go,
Daddy whispers, soft and low:

"Sweet dreams...
Sleep tight...
Love you morning,
Noon, and night."